To Helen Smith and her son, Luke, who
appears as the boy in these pages, and to the
memory of his father, Captain Lucas. You
were, and always will be, my favorite captain.

Thanks to Bobby, Kristin, and Keenan
Cummings for their time and effort.
You guys are the best!

Published by Familius LLC, www.familius.com

Familius books are available at special discounts for bulk purchases for sales promotions, family
or corporate use. Special editions, including personalized covers, excerpts of existing books,
or books with corporate logos, can be created in large quantities for special needs. For more
information, contact Premium Sales at 559-876-2170 or email specialmarkets@familius.com.

Library of Congress Catalog-in-Publication Data

2014940271

ISBN 978-1-939629-28-9

Cover and book design by David Miles

10 9 8 7 6 5 4 3 2 1

First Edition

# the STICK

## by Clay Rice

 FAMILIUS

Once there was a boy
who had no toys to play
with. The other children in the
neighborhood had lots of toys.
Every afternoon, the boy would
go to the park, sit under a big tree,
and watch the other children play.
Sometimes they let the boy play
with their toys. Sometimes not.

This made the boy sad.

O ne day, as the boy was sitting under the big tree in the park, he noticed a stick leaning against the trunk. He had never seen such an unusual stick. He picked it up.

Suddenly, he was a

PIRATE!

Then a baseball player at bat.

And then a knight on a steed.

The boy noticed that
there were words carved
into the stick. He sang
them like a song:

IMAGINATION
lives in you.
It's the FIRE
in all you do.
Use it well, and
you can be
ANYTHING
you want
to be.

The boy carried the stick everywhere, and anywhere he was, he was anything he wanted to be.

At the beach, he was a fisherman.
At the lake, he paddled a canoe.
He was a hiker in the highlands.
And his imagination grew.

Time passed, and the boy grew up. With the stick's inspiration, he became everything he wanted to be.

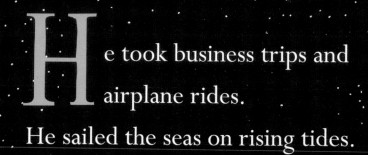

He took business trips and
airplane rides.
He sailed the seas on rising tides.

He gave of his time.
He gave of his wealth.
He gave from his heart.
He gave of himself.

He built a house high on a hill, overlooking the valley where he had grown up.

In the distance, he
could see the park
and the old tree
where he used to sit.

As the years passed, the boy became an old man. But each day, he took his stick with him to the park and sat on a bench near the tree where he had found the stick so long ago.

He would sit for hours and watch the children play.

All of the children seemed to have lots of toys to play with—except for one little girl.

The little girl always sat under the old tree and watched the other children play with their toys. This made the old man sad.

Early one morning, the old man walked to the park, but instead of sitting on the bench, he went over to the tree. He leaned the stick against its trunk, walked to his bench, and waited.

Soon, the children arrived at the park with their toys. He waited to see if the little girl would show. He saw her walk slowly toward the tree. She peered down at the unusual stick leaning against its trunk.

She picked up the stick, and suddenly . . .

. . . she was a princess!

A fencer.

Then a surfer riding a wave.

She noticed that there were words carved into the stick, and as she danced away, she sang them like a song:

# IMAGINATION lives in you.

It's the FIRE in all you do. Use it well, and you can be ANYTHING you want to be.

And the old man smiled
and walked home.